Copyright © 2

This is a work of fiction based loosely on family legend. ... the names have been changed to protect the identites of the family.

ISBN: 9798839661936
Imprint: Independently published

Thanks to my partner and to Jan for being great sounding boards and proof readers.

PREFACE

A soldier mentioned in dispatches is one whose name appears in an offical report due to brave actions in conflict.

My Great Grandad was mentioned in dispatches and what I know of the story has always fascinated me. I am not an expert on the war, nor do I know my Great Grandad's story so I have written a work of fiction based on some family legends and my imagination.

John Kelly

Belgium 1917

When it comes, and I knew it would come, it hit me before I even realised it was on its way. A head shot. I lie on the floor in a crumpled heap. I'm so thin that I look like a discarded uniform. If you don't notice my head that is.

The burying party come. I recognise one of them, Lynch. We grew up together in Ireland. Ah the skies of home; they're a far cry from these sodden clouds of Flanders. We were used to rain and wind alright but it wasn't like this muddy hell.

Lynch and I met up in England a couple of years ago, ended up in the same regiment, and here we are. I suppose you could say things are going better for him than me. Although I will no longer have to put up with the hunger, the rats, the rotting clothing and the rotten feet. I'll soon be part of the God-awful stench of this stinking Belgian mud.

I think of my wife and my children as my body is dug into the treacherous cloying ground. The time that's passed since I last saw 'em, like a great black chasm; filled with death and despair. I pray they are safe and that they stay that way.

William Jones

Palestine 1917

Dust clings to my boots as I walk slowly towards what is left of the stables. The whinnying carries across on the wind and greets me before I can return the greeting. I hope they're not wanting much in the way of breakfast, there's not much here to feed them on.

I nod at a group of men as they walk past me. I don't know their names. I don't want to know. I focus on the small hard bottle in my pocket. Shame it's almost empty.

The unlucky horses who live outside observe me with large baleful eyes, their hooves, and coats thick with sand. They stamp with impatience, and I pat them in turn, stroking their dirty flanks and speak to them in a soft calm voice.

Sitting in the relative protection of the stable I take out the bottle of rum; there's precious little left, but I sip at it and feel the warmth spread like sunshine through my body. I put the bottle away, my dirty hands shake as I button up my jacket. I have no breakfast either; like the horses we're short on rations.

I look around at the poor beasts and my stomach twists. I think of the forge back home in Polesworth; the horses stamping their feet and the bird nesting in the pocket of my great coat, the rum, and the brown ale I kept on the shelf, and the fire, permanently lit. There's always breakfast there, for me and for them and not just the liquid variety.

'Bill.' says a stern voice behind me. I look around although I recognise the grim tones.

'Harold.' I reply. 'Any news? These animals are starving.'

'They can't get through Bill. There's some sawdust we can add to what's left; fill up their stomachs,' Harold suggests although the look on his face tells me he knows I'm far from impressed. Harold had a hard face at the at the best of times but today his lean, square jaw was set. The redness on his face decorated with a bristly moustache and a thatch of brown hair.

'Would it fool you if it was in your rations?' I ask sharply, looking up at him. I should have stood up; he was my superior officer but was a good three inches shorter than me. He stood still, almost enjoying his greater height for once; he looked down at me for a second before replying.

'No Bill, but it might stop my stomach complaining for a while,' He said and he marches away into the bright biting sun.

I sigh and look at the horses closest to me. Some had only just got over pneumonia, having become ill on the journey overseas. Poor sods, so many horses were well loved before being brought out here to die.

'And won't we be on the move soon?' I shout after him. 'They can't pull anything on empty stomachs.'

After breakfast I start cleaning them and prepare to clip them, as instructed in the pamphlet. Nonsense if you ask me; but nobody did, so I follow orders. I can't argue with everything. I am only a Farrier Sergeant after all. Despite starting just after dawn, I look up at the sky as I finish clipping the final horse and am surprised to see another dusk settling on the landscape. The day had passed in a blur of sand, horsehair, and worry. I can't see that tomorrow would be any better.

A few minutes later, having put away the meagre equipment I stroke each horse again, saying their names in turn as I touch them.

"Buck, Nelson, Sandy, Captain, Shade." and admire the harnessed strength in their flanks, the soft strong muzzles, and their soulful eyes. There'll be at least one that is lifeless in the morning. Or worse, there will be at least one that I will have to put out of its misery. I dread the dawn.

Mary Kelly

England 1917

The grate has been blacked, clothes scrubbed, floors swept, and the children are out playing. I stand and look at the only picture of John, the one over which I pray for his safe return every day since he left. His dark hair cut short, partially hidden by his hat which sat casting a shadow over his nose. His eyes bore into me, accusing me as I go about the daily tasks that I loathe. There was a twinkle there too, in his eyes. 'Come on Mary,' they said, 'don't take so.'

'It's alright for you,' I tell him, my voice hard, 'you could leave, I have to stay, there's no avoiding it for me.' Letters come occasionally; I read them and then put them safe, in the box under my bed, to re-read on days when nothing comes, and the rain pours down the tears that I refuse to cry. Let the earth cry for this.

Then it comes. Like a shell from no man's land. Anticipated yet unexpected.

The girls watch as I take the paper from the boy. They eye me with interest but know better than to ask yet and they carry on playing. I go back inside. I sit down at the scrubbed table in the small dark kitchen. I can hear them in the yard. Enid and little Mary squealing and giggling. Sarah trying to sing a nursery rhyme, but she doesn't know the words.

The paper shakes in my hand. He promised to come back. 'Ring a ring o roses', skips through my brain as Sarah, outside, hums the first two lines over and over.

A pocket full of posies. The flowers he gave me when he left have been dead a long time. Bastard. John had freedom, he could make choices, even if sometimes they were bloody stupid choices. I was always frightened he would leave me for good.

A tissue, a tissue. I feel overwhelmed. Can I cope alone?

We all fall down. A tear rolls down my face; I sit still in the chair. There's no point in moving; there's nothing to do. It ain't raining outside; but I cry now. The downpour is mine.

John is dead. He has fallen down, well and truly. He's in the trenches, buried in the filthy Belgian mud, with the broken bones and rotting flesh of the others who had been killed before him. All those angry wives and all those bloody men, gone, as if they never existed, but for the little ones running around in their grubby trousers and dresses, smiling up with their father's mouths or begging for more food with his pleading face.

I pick up his photo and hurl it at the floor. My anger splinters along with the glass. I cry sharp bitter tears while I sweep up the mess and replace the broken picture on the side.

Sarah stops singing. I don't want to hear singing ever again.

The future stretches out bleak and worn like the table.

John Kelly

1917

Mary is practical. She cleans, cooks, runs the house with a strict routine and God forbid anything that doesn't fit in with it, so I'm not worried about the house, or there not being food on the table, she would do that alright. It's the other stuff. The warm twinkle of a caring pair of eyes, the sympathy of a thoughtful question, the helpfulness of a considered answer; these things I know she can't do. If I could cry, I would weep for Enid, little Mary and Sarah, who may as well be here with me for all the warmth they'll get at home.

The war is still going on around me, men are dying in their thousands from West to East Flanders, and into France. It's a blood bath but they're still trying, holding back the Germans. Odd that it should just continue. Or right I suppose, who am I? A man, an Irishman. I'm of no consequence; just like the thousands of others. And now I can't protect my country, my fellow soldiers, or my children.

But do I regret going? Ah, what else would I have done? There was no work, and I had to leave after the riots in Swords and the lockout. This had been sommat, and Mary had been pleased enough with the shillings, so she had. She had known when we left home that was the plan. No point crying over it now. I doubt she will though, cry that is. I never knew her to; not even when the worst happened. She's a tough old bird. She'll be busy finding a solution. That's what my Mary'll do. She'll find a solution.

William Jones

Palestine 1917

The warm air invites me out to the stables despite the early hour. Some men are chatting, some re-reading letters from home that are filthy and torn from being pulled out of pockets, read in the dirt, and shoved hurriedly back in.

I have no letters and I don't care for chatter. I trudge away from my fellow soldiers and stride as purposefully as I can towards the stable area. The sound of the horses carries on the warm wind, it reassures me a bit, but my stomach tenses as I get closer; their rations filled out with sawdust would not have done much for them yesterday.

I see it before I get there. One horse, on the floor. Buck. At least that's all, I had dreaded it being worse. I groan as I drop to the earth to sit beside him. I stroke his still belly. My hand shakes as I stroke him over and over. Did he know I loved him? I question as I bury my face in his downy coat. I hope he had a nice life before he came here. I close my eyes and imagine him on an American farm, his muscles rippling as he canters around the fields, chestnut mane long and well brushed. His hooves had been well cared for, for all the good it's done him now. I wonder if he missed home, or his people?

A vision of my home drifts into my mind. I can see the green village square just down from my forge, the white frothy river Anker with the pretty stone bridge, the Chequers Inn on the corner. It all seems so peaceful now from a distance. I don't think of the noise or the people but sitting here quietly, I can feel the gentle breeze from the river brush my face and ruffle my hair with the familiar touch of home.

Some soldier or other walks up to me, his boots kick up a spray of dust. I'm reluctantly brought back to now.

'Bill,' he says, as if it was a question. I open my eyes but don't look up. It's Harold.

'No.' The conversation is over as far as I'm concerned.

'Bill, the men are hungry,' he insists.

'So are the God damn horses,' I spit.

'Bill, they ain't people you know.'

'And I'm damn grateful for that,' I reply honestly.

More feet arrive; black, brown, dusty, torn. Some limping over, some hobbling, the new ones walking with a confidence they probably don't feel, but there they are in front of me. Determined.

I drag myself up and look up into the face of Harold. His sunburned face is grimy, and his cheeks are hollowed out like bullet wounds. His wild hair stands on end. The moustache that sat under his nose watched me as surely as his steely grey eyes.

'I'm burying him,' I say firmly, 'it's the least he deserves.'

'William--,'

'Don't William me, he's worked damn hard during this war and on low rations. He deserves a burial, same as you and I,' I hold his gaze and the men around us shift on their tired feet; torn between hunger and a fight.

'He deserves, he deserves!' explodes out from behind his moustache which is now waving furiously at me, signalling his exasperation. 'What has deserving got to do with anything? We don't deserve this!' He gestures at the ragged men and the barren surroundings with his arm, 'But without him,' he stops and looks at the dead horse, 'men will starve. Is that what you want, Sergeant?'

I look around at the men standing with their arms folded, the hunger seems to reach out of their pathetic bedraggled bodies. Their faces echo the sentiments that have just been spoken. They don't need to join in; I'm on my own.

I can't look as they take him away. The feet retreat slowly but there is an air of excitement, triumph almost. The men are happy to be getting a meal. A young private named South, spits on the ground in front of me before he walks off, his black boots drag in the sand, his upper lip curled. It could be the sand in his mouth, or it could be contempt. I don't really care which. After a minute or two I look up to see a short young man with a dirty mop of blond hair who has remained behind. He looks back at me without saying a word then reaches inside his pocket; his hand comes back out clasped around a familiar bottle. He takes a step towards me.

'Bill,' he says softly, his eyes look up to mine and I'm surprised to see he has tears just about to begin their journey through the grime on his thin face. He places the rum in the shaking hand I put out to meet his.

<u>Mary Kelly</u>

<u>England 1917</u>

'Come in 'ere with that rag Mary,' I demand sharply. Where is that girl? She is never quite where I want her to be.

'Sarah, Enid I continue no less sharply, just because they're young don't mean they can dilly dally.

The three girls clatter into the room all at once. Sarah starts to make a noise that sounds suspiciously like the first note of ring a ring o roses.

'Enough,' I snap. Their small faces look pinched. Their eyes fix on me, round and large in the tightly covered bones.

'Have you cleaned the room?' I look carefully at them as I wait for an answer. You have to watch 'em; sneaky they are. They have beautiful names though, don't they? Me and John had made sure of that, beautiful names. But a name could hide the devil himself and these three could have an evil streak alright. John, he is soft, had been soft, I correct myself but there'll be no getting away with things now. They nodded, in unison, a sure sign the job has not been done if ever I saw one. I sigh.

'Enid take this and get a loaf of bread from Bond's; make sure it's fresh.' I hand her a small coin, not sure where the next one will come from.

'Little Mary, you go with her.' I turn back to the papers in the drawer that I was sorting. A few seconds later I look up in surprise as I realise that no one has moved. "Were you not given an instruction? What in the name of heaven are ye waiting for?' My eyebrows raised up, synchronised with my voice which was now at least an octave higher than usual. The girls should know by now this signals danger.

'Ma,' Enid begins, 'the letter—you haven't told us yet…,' her blue eyes beg me for news.

'He's not coming back, he's dead.' no point stringing it out. Her face drops. Little Mary and Sarah look at each other, then at Enid who throws herself down at the table, her tears spill carelessly onto the exhausted wood. Sarah climbs up onto her lap, her small pale hands grab at her neck. Little Mary starts to sob too, spurred on by her sisters' reactions.

'Sitting crying won't help,' I sniff, 'go and get the bread before there's none left or all you'll be 'aving for tea is cabbage water; and there's no breakfast neither.'

Later, the pepper stung my eyes as I shook it into the pale thin fluid. The girls drank in silence. They dip their bread and then swallow it in haste, like someone's going to take it away. We stare at the two empty chairs, and they stare back, unblinking. We sit motionless, all four of us, eyes smarting, sucking up the meal as if it were our last.

William Jones

Palestine 1917

I turn and vomit again, spitting bitter bile onto the earth, clutching my stomach. As soon as I can bear to let go my hand shoots out to search for the bottle that I'd dropped in the dirt a minute before. My eyes stream as I forage blindly. The aroma on the air seemed to fill every atom, taunting me without mercy. It made my nausea bloom. Flames, smoke, and slowly roasting meat.

The laughter of the men dances over on the stench of their feast. I hope they choke on it. I'd rather eat the sawdust we fed the horses. At least the horses have dignity which was more than I can say for that lot. What next? Will they eat the men that drop down dead? I shudder at that thought although I muse that it repulses me only slightly less than the thought of eating a horse. You know where you are with a horse, there's no secret agenda and there's a lot to be said for something that can't argue back. I've had many a good conversation with my horses. They don't come up with bloody ridiculous ideas either.

I look over at Harold. He's holding court, throwing his arms out and laughing loudly. His stance says, 'look at me, I've given you all a good meal,' I turn and spit. Smug bastard. He won't be so smug in a few days' time when he realises that we're trapped will he? What will he do then? Carry us out himself! Harold turns as if he knows I am looking, he has the audacity to smile at me, but it looks more like a grimace in the firelight.

To my surprise the lad with the dirty blond hair starts walking over, he slows down as he gets close, as if he wished he hadn't started. I look around, there's nothing and no one nearby so he can't pretend he was going somewhere else.

'Alright lad,' I offer. I hadn't forgotten the rum.

'Ay, mind if I sit Sergeant?'

'As long as you haven't brought your supper with you.'

He sat, stretching his legs out in front of him.

'Nah,' he looked up at me 'I didn't much fancy it, I mean, I know we're hungry and all that but…' He trailed off.

I nodded.

'Sir, Sgt Jones,' he dug his hands in the dirt and gave a brief glance over at the men by the fire before continuing. 'I wondered--I wondered if you wanted to check the horses early. In the morning I mean, just in case--I thought we could--' he drifted off with a slight shrug.

'What's your name son?'

'Cooper Sir, Private Cooper.'

I felt my muscles relax and form the first genuine smile I had felt in a long time.

'Reckon we could,' I passed him the rum. 'Bloody great idea, I reckon we could.'

It was early as we creep over to the horses, but there is still enough ink in the sky to give us some cover. I feel glad for the dark when we get there; I hope it covers the great blossoming stain of agony that is taking over my body and I know is written on my face. Cooper sits down heavily.

'Sergeant, I'm so sorry,' He says quietly. He gets up and leaves. I wipe my face with my coarse sleeve, taking care not to make my eyes any more red. I look down at Nelson, Sandy and Captain. They look drained and smaller somehow than yesterday.

I think he is just giving me a minute with the horses, but he comes back holding two shovels. Without a word, I take one off him and together we start to dig.

It's hard work but I am used to it and so it seems is the lad.

'What did you do? before this I mean.'

'Grew up on a farm, could've stayed, but I wanted to come and fight, do my bit.' he looked at me almost apologetically.

'Your dad at home still on the farm?'

'Yes, he delivers the milk, has big shire horses, beautiful proud creatures.' Cooper's eyes shine as he says this. I can imagine them, huge, solid bulks in stunning colours, pulling a cart with an attractive man reminiscent of young Cooper sitting behind.

'Has he not got help now you've left?'

'I'm one of seven,' Cooper explained. 'There's three of us sons and four daughters so they have enough help at home. Anyway, I'm not dad's favourite, he won't miss me so much.'

'Well, you seem like a good lad to me,' I tell him honestly. 'Your parents must have done something right.'

'Ah my dad is quite soft really, well with the others. It's me mam who kept us all in line; literally. She lined us all up once as she found a plum in the garden with a bite out of it, and she wanted to compare our teeth to the marks in the plum.' He laughs, shaking his blond head.

'Did she find the culprit?'

'Our Fred ended up with a right tanning as me mam swore his teeth matched but he won't admit it to this day.' He grins at me. I join in with his laughter then stop when I realise what we are still doing. Sobered we carry on digging.

South wanders into view. He had the same look on

his face as the day he spat at my feet. He didn't say anything, nor offer to help. He just stood smoking and watching. We didn't acknowledge his presence either. No doubt he would soon be reporting us. They'd have realised the horses were gone soon enough anyhow.

South wanders away and Cooper pauses in his shovelling.

'What if he reports us?'

'See any other Farriers around here?' I ask

'No, but there's not many horses either Bill, what if he puts us on a charge?' Cooper throws down his spade. 'Bloody hell this is all my fault.'

I lean on my spade and wipe the sweat off my face. 'We've done the right thing, whatever the consequences, console yourself with that lad.' I can't say any more. There's nothing more to say.

<u>Mary Kelly</u>

<u>England 1917</u>

The girls are quiet before bed, but then they know better than to make unnecessary noise. I'm glad to get them off to bed, time for me to think. So, I think, and all I can think is that it seems there's no luck for the men in this family, or the women for that matter. I'm glad to get to bed meself, although God only knows there's no hope for a better day tomorrow. It feels like minutes later, but is surely hours, when a noise screeches out and cuts through the darkness like a sharp knife.

'Ma, ma,' a pause, 'Ma. I'm awake straight away and I tread carefully on the cold floorboards as I blindly make my way to the source of the sound, heart pounding. I can feel my blood rushing round my body. My stomach lurches and my head spins. I can taste acid. Calm down Mary, I coax myself, come on. It's alright. I draw in a deep breath and stand up as full as my inconsiderable height allows.

'What on earth is all this racket? Enid Kelly is that you?' I peer into the darkness, searching for part of a human face. A small hand reaches out. I push it away to light a candle. It is Enid, her dark curls wild, eyes large, pupils even larger as they seek out a thread of light. Her little chest is heaving pathetically, like the rib cage of a delicate bird.

'Ma, was it the flames?' she asks with a cry before starting to wail hysterically. 'Oh it was the flames, I know it was,' she continued, her voice trembling now the same as her body. Sarah and little Mary are sitting up, they look at Enid in fear, then at me, as if waiting for an answer.

Enid hadn't had a nightmare for a good while. I had been hoping she wouldn't have them regularly again, we have enough to contend with. Mind you, her fear of fire was not easy to manage in a house full of candles.

I sigh, wait a second to see if she stops, then when she doesn't, I put out my hand and slap her hard around the face. She gasps sharply and looked at me in horror.

'Ma,' she whispered.

'That stopped your ridiculous noise Enid Kelly, there's just no need now is there?' Little Mary and Sarah shrink back, as if wanting to remove themselves from this spectacle.

Enid sniffed and rubbed at her cheek.

'Sorry Ma, I just had that dream, only this time it was Da.' she paused and took in a shaky breath. 'Was it flames that killed him Ma?'

'No, it wasn't the flames. It was war; just war.' I say although realise that I may burn in the flames, but in hell for all eternity, as I have no idea what the actual truth of the matter was.

'The Vicar says right will prevail,' little Mary leans in. 'Will it Ma?'

'Of course, it will now go back to sleep. We can't change anything. No good crying over spilt milk is there now,.' I blow out the candle carefully, not enjoying the thick smoky smell that follows me like a ghost as I begin shuffling back to my room before anyone can object.

My room. It's odd to think of it without John, that he won't ever return. We had some good times, and the heart-breaking ones too. It's only natural I suppose. But what's natural now? Men gone to war. Women and children alone and hungry. When is it ever going to end?

The old bed creaks as I lie back down, it sounds like me, complaining at life and worn down with poverty and the empty hunger that grasps at us pulling us down, hastening our journey to the earth.

Ashes in the water.

I lie down, thinking of John and of Patrick, but I don't cry again.

William Jones

Palestine 1917

Cooper passes me a cigarette and we smoke in silence for a while. The near desolate stables watch us with questioning eyes, as if asking us what we are going to do next.

'What'll we do then?' Cooper echoes the desolate landscape.

It's the question on all our minds. We are sitting targets, there's an approaching enemy and we can't get away, not with all the equipment. To leave it would be madness.

'Perhaps we shudda fed the men to the horses instead of the other way round,' I say half joking. 'Then we'd have had a couple of beasts to help us and less people to feed to boot.'

Cooper laughs and flicks his hair, gently dragging his hands across his forehead. His blue eyes were clear and open, and I felt he could see inside me in a way I couldn't with him. He was so young. I hadn't looked for this companionship but now I don't want to do without it. Cooper is the only thing, along with the horses, that keeps me sane out here. I wonder what will happen when this is over? If we get out alive, will we ever see each other again?

Cooper looks out across the bleak terrain, oblivious to my musings. His blond hair whips up and down in the wind, his fine bronzed features focus on the huge nothingness before us. He looks trouble free. I guess no one was accusing him of stealing plums out here. He's not the usual soldier type at all, he's quiet and seems delicate. I tear my eyes away as I hear footsteps approaching.

'Sergeant Jones,' a soldier clears his throat. 'Captain wants to see you immediately,' The soldier looks at us then he turns and marches away, back towards to the tents.

I pull myself up, my long legs already towering over Cooper. He glances up. He looks almost God like lying there in the sun. Ironic that we're at war, yet he looks like the closest thing to a reclining angel I have ever seen.

'I'll be back,' I said in a subdued voice, 'I hope.' I threw over my shoulder as an afterthought as I made my way to the captain's tent. This was surely not going to be good news. He's probably going to sacrifice the horse for the last supper.

Harold greets me with a grunt which I take to mean good morning and he gestures to a chair. I sit without returning his greeting.

'Jones,' he starts, 'as you know our situation is dire. We have only one horse remaining, and we need to move the men and the guns.'

'Ay,' This is not news to me, what did he expect me to say?

'Is that all you have to say? He questions. 'You're the Farrier sergeant, horses are your remit.'

I raise an eyebrow.

'Is that so?' I say, my voice low and dangerous.

'While they're alive Jones. I haven't forgotten your little trick last week, they're army property after all,' he says, his voice snakelike and treacherous. 'But let's get back to the business in hand. We have a problem,' he insists.

'It's not exactly news, Sir.' I try to look him in the eyes, but he won't keep them still. His fingers tap on the table at odds with the rhythm of his knee which bounces up and down under the desk.

'I do have a solution, actually,' I add.

He stills and meets my gaze for the first time since he took the dead horse.

'Go on.' He surveys me with interest.

'I'll go and get some horses; I'll take theirs,' I announce with more confidence than I feel. 'Have you got any cigarettes?'

Harold pulls a packet from his pocket and hands it to me.

'You make it sound so easy Bill,' he says eyeing me as I take a smoke. 'Taking enemy horses will be no mean feat.'

I shrug.

'No point making a fuss about it. I'll go and get some horses, bring 'em back here. Then we can move.'

'Who do you want to take with you?'

I take a puff on the cigarette and screw up my eyes.

'I don't want no one; prefer to be on my own.'

'I know you do Bill, but I think you should have someone with you,' he pauses and absentmindedly picks up a pencil, he twirls it in between his fingers and looks down at his desk. 'How about--Cooper?' he says, looking me directly in the eyes.

John Kelly

1917

Watching Mary with the candle in the night makes me shudder. I never liked candles after the events of 1912, and it wasn't the same at home neither. A sadness settled with the ash, and we couldn't shift it long after the ash had been cleared away. Mary, who had been taciturn before, became even more dour. If the war hadn't started, I don't know what we'd have done. It saved us I guess, as divorce was out of the question.

The girls were young thank God, although Enid never forgot. She had doted on Patrick and stroked his little curls while he slept, patting his rosy cheeks, and singing him nursery rhymes. Ring a ring o' roses was a favourite, I chuckle at the memory, she sang it to Sarah too when she was born as I remember.

Little Mary don't remember though, thank God, being only a year older than Patrick herself. Thankfully she was toddling outside with her ma and Enid when it happened. Ah I don't blame Mary; it was an accident. And to be honest, I don't know if she blames herself. I never asked. Still, I'll be around, I'll always watch over my girls

Everything was black and scorched, ashes blowing about in the wind, settling on the river below and making their escape out to sea.

Ashes in the water, Ashes in the sea.

She's got less mouths to feed now I s'pose.

<u>William Jones</u>

Palestine 1917

We sit with our backs against the wheels, we pass the rum between us and share a smoke.

'I come from a small place, in the middle of nowhere. I can't believe that I am in a place like this,' Cooper says as if he has only just realised, he is not at home.

'It's just the same though, isn't it?

Cooper looks at me, mouth hanging open, eyes wide.

'The same! Well, let's see at home its wet and cold mostly. Here it's hotter than your forge and as dry as parchment.' he looked at me as if willing me to understand, 'and there's no women,' then adds 'nor stores.'

'Cooper, the way I look at it is people are people and animals are animals wherever they are; it's exactly the same.' I take a large gulp of rum and wonder briefly if I should drink tea some of the time.

'Maybe you're right Sergeant, maybe you're right.'

'You keen to see a woman are you, Cooper?'

'Oh no,' his cheeks turned pink under the bronze, 'I can do without women. I was just saying that's all.'

'It's a darn sight more peaceful I reckon without women, although.' I nod my head over in the direction of Harold. 'there's always one fly in the ointment.'

Cooper laughs, then turns to me, his face serious and sad.

'It's just, I can't be myself at home. That's how I feel anyway. My dad--my dad--he thinks I'm--funny. That I'm not manly enough," He looked up at me from under his eyelashes, he looks sheepish, guilty almost. 'I was so lonely,' he continued 'even in a busy house. I came out here because I thought I might feel less lonely. I haven't even had a reply to my letters home,' he concludes and then a sob escapes his downturned mouth.

I grab at him and pull him into my chest and my arms cradle his heaving body; his mop of blond hair sits just under my chin. I feel his hands place themselves gently on my back.

....

An aroma of sweat and dirt forces its way through my fog of sleep, at first, I can't work out why it is different to the usual smell that assaults me on waking, but then I see Cooper. God, he looks young when he sleeps.

Straightening my uniform, I step outside the

tent. The air is never really fresh here, but it feels it after the fug of male scents in the small, enclosed space.

I go straight to see Harold; we need to talk through the details of tonight. There's not much to say really, I just need to be clear about directions. If it goes wrong, then so be it.

The maps were creased and worn, but we could make sense of them well enough.

'Still feeling sure about this Bill?' Harold enquired

'Yes,' I insisted, 'we need some horses, its got to work.'

Harold nodded.

'Get yourself ready,' he said.

An ear-splitting boom brought the meeting to a sudden end. The ground seemed to shake and everything around us erupted. We raced outside on legs that shook but still carried us towards the chaos. Men ran and dove for weapons and for safety. Sand flew, attacking us and shielding us simultaneously as it swung a thick curtain through the air. Men fired back indiscriminately; grenades were thrown into the zone of blind combat. My gun protested at the sand and spluttered before eventually took its orders and fired rounds out in front of me.

I have no idea how long it continued but eventually we are left alone with the blood, the dead, and ears buzzing from the noise that had withdrawn as quickly as it had arrived. I sit surveying the mess, nothing much is recognisable, until I see a familiar dirty blond head, face down on the floor.

<u>Mary Kelly</u>

<u>England 1917</u>

The ripped nail looks forlorn on the end of my reddened fingers. I wonder if my hands would ever be free of work. Mary, Sarah, and Enid are at school. I have nothing to do but tidying, cleaning, and wondering how I will feed them for the rest of the week. The remainder of the nail, the free part was on the end of my tongue, I enjoy the pricking of pain as I push it into the gum above my front tooth; there was another on already in there. Later, I will manipulate them back out with my tongue too. The quick burst of pain a relief from the everyday worries.

I thought about the work I have heard about. It would mean leaving Enid in charge in a morning, but better that than starve. The girls looked thin, and I know that I do too. Not that we have ever been large, but our dresses are hanging off us like limp rags loosely draped on a family of skeletons.

The picture of John looked on with disapproval, the jagged pieces of glass like weapons against his face. I don't want to look at it. I know he would not like me leaving the children but what else can I do? I could always re-marry, not that there are many men to choose from now, with them all away at war.

I'm fed up with the stories of war and of the death that follows them through life like a sinister shadow. I feel the shadow's coldness on my back as I look at the empty chairs. I shiver and tweak the fingernail with my tongue.

Digging out the vegetables in the garden reminds me of digging a grave, but I remove the precious food with care. The garden has some things still growing thank God. It was a scruffy patch of land that ran from the fence to the side of the house, lining the top of the cellar with a collar of soil, topped off with bags of sand.

The cellar is a godsend, a comfort blanket, even though it was damp, dark, and it smells like the soil outside which at least makes us feel free when were in there. Later that evening we go to the cellar when the noises come. When it is so loud that any thoughts of grief or life are obliterated. We rush down, sleepy, rubbing our eyes with one hand, a pillow, and a blanket in the other. The girls don't move quickly enough, and I am half dragging someone as we try to leave the noise and danger behind. The girls' tears punctuate the coming and going of the engines and the candle flickers despair onto the bare brick.

A few days later, I start work at the farm the other side of the village. I leave in the half light, but I wake Enid before I exit the house with an instruction that she is not to light any candles. She nods at me with a serious face. I know I don't need to tell her why. The recent nightmare lingers between our rumbling stomachs and the vacant chairs. A reminder of our frailty.

John Kelly

<u>1917</u>

Our three girls, left alone so early in a morning. I shudder with fear. Anything could happen. Thank God Enid is sensible enough or scared enough to do as her mam says. God-willing they keep getting to school safe. At least Mary is there when they come home and they have more to eat now she's working, I'll gi' her that.

I worry about her mixing with new people but the family on the farm look a decent sort. Strict, hardworking and they pay fair wages. She is still getting to Church with the girls which is good, I don't want her cut off from everyone, not at this time of need. The girls need friends an 'all. They need sommat to make 'em smile while they're living with Mary. I wish I could blow down a warm breeze for 'em sometimes, cloak 'em with it to keep 'em safe. I couldn't keep Patrick safe either. I thought I'd see him again one day but there's nowt here. It's as barren as a desert. I hope to see his plump little face and cuddle him again. But death has turned out to be as pointless as life was for me.

<u>William Jones</u>

<u>Palestine 1917</u>

I stand useless outside the tent. I hadn't noticed my own wound until I had pulled Cooper away from the tangled mess of bodies and earth. It was nothing serious, so I've been bandaged up and sent out of the way. I have a smoke and wait. Cooper is still inside.

Harold marches past. Eyes serious. He walks in without a word.

It's hot today, and the danger of our situation has been emphasised by the events that took place earlier. We need to move and attack from a new position. The new horses are more important than ever. My left arm throbs with pain but it's nothing I can't put up with.

Harold comes back out and stands next to me.

'Cooper will be moved, he needs proper treatment,' he says then pauses, still looking at me. 'South can go with you, tonight.'

I nod, we need the horses to move Cooper. Whatever South feels about me and me for him, we are on the same side after all.

'Sir.' I nod and walk away. I had little time to get prepared, but I didn't need much. Weapons, rope, and my wits should be enough.

It felt like minutes later that we were ready. The

rest of the platoon were ready to attack from their position; meanwhile we were to sneak through, find the horses and come back with them.

The men charged; grenades and bullets assaulted the air, ripping through the silken dark of late evening. We made slow progress from our position; low to the ground, South with his gun raised, ready each time we paused. Not having much to go home to, I feel less nervous than some would, what did it really matter if I was hit? Killed? Who would mourn? Maybe there will be someone when, if, I ever get home. Some days I think I would like a wife. I can't stand the thought of a soppy, clingy woman though, or someone who will lean on me too much. Maybe there will be some independent women after the war. There won't be as many men that's for sure.

I shake my head. It's not about me. I need to succeed for them, the other soldiers, and to get Cooper to safety.

We crawl and stop, crawl and stop, the sounds of battle still loud but not as frighteningly close. We finally reach relative safety. The men are all forward, their horses out of the way like ours used to be. There are some men left, we need to get rid of them. South and I pick a place where we can shoot and hopefully remain undetected, where we can move on from.

My hands are sweating now, not just from the heat, but the need for this work. I don't want to dissolve into the sand and be no-one's memory.

Lying on the ground, distant sounds of violence seem to echo the throb of my pulse. I doubt I'd hear if anyone approached but my ears are straining all the same, dreading the tread of a boot, or the click of a gun, or worse, the sound of one being fired.

There are two men by the stables, more might come running when we shoot, but we have to act, we can't walk down as things are. I look over at South, he is tense, his gun steady against his shoulder, he motions to me that he's ready. I look over in the direction he is pointing his gun, his eyes fixed on a soldier. I turn and get ready to fire too. Every grain of sand, strand of grass, and buzzing insect seems to be waiting too, the air, full and dense breathes in with us. I nod at him, and after a split-second we fire, not quite in unison, but with no time in between the shots for anyone to react. The soldiers slump to the floor. I don't know if the rush is in the air or in my body and before anything else can happen, we move, slowly, but we move; in case a watching soldier has been made aware of our position and a retaliating bullet is on its way.

There is no movement, no bullet, and no blood where we are lying, panting with nerves and adrenaline. We move closer inch by inch, noiseless actions; every sound of the night makes our hairs stand on end, our eyes large with fear. Looking hard through the night our eyes focus on the soldiers, the area around them, and the roughly constructed stable area from where the familiar and comforting sound of horses' hooves and snorts emanate.

We dare to stand, the booms and shots in the background reassure us that most of the enemy soldiers are busy. We make our way towards the shelter, aware of every placement of our boots, the noise they make on the sand, rasping and scratchy sounds unbearably loud even with the background noise from the battle.

The darkness is like a cloak now but still we would be seen if someone came to the horses. Sweat trickles down my face, South is looking around warily, our guns are poised. The shelter is twenty feet away, I am dizzy with relief and excitement, we could do this. Another crunching noise is added to our medley, I see a pair of scuffed boots, a muddied trouser leg, and the tip of a rifle. I look up, surprised that at this point we have met an obstacle, I had thought we were there, well halfway there at least.

He is smoking, and looks relaxed, I am not sure he registers that we aren't on his side. He smiles and speaks. I have no idea what he is saying. In response I raise my gun and wave him away. A look of confusion passes over his face. He starts to lift his gun, then he pauses.

I put my hands down, shaking, my gun still smoking, South is behind me, his gun ready but not needed. The soldier is on the floor, his smile sinking into the sand along with his blood; black, in the darkness.

"Come on Bill," South urges.

I hesitated. It had been close range, he smiled at us. Why?

"Bill." South tugs at my sleeve.

I turn away from the mess on the floor and head into the stable area. South and I turn to each other and smile briefly. Then we set to work.

Despite our poor rations, the nerves, and the adrenaline, we manage to attach ropes to the horses quickly. Jubilance is building despite me warning myself that it isn't okay yet. With fumbling fingers, I tie off the end of the rope. The horses respond to having company, they stamp and whinny and seem keen to move.

A croft crunching noise outside alerts us to danger. My gun is ready, South is poised too, and we fire simultaneously as an unsuspecting soldier comes into view. He falls without ceremony.

'We need to start moving George,' I tell South

South nods, I move to the front and take the halter of the horse at the front. We begin our wary journey out into the open.

We are so big and unwieldy, and we make slow progress; it seems incredible that half of the enemy troops don't unleash hell onto our back as we head towards our own area of relative safety, but they don't. They must all be at the front, maybe the noise is helping us, maybe the moon is looking away, shining on something else, allowing us to make our escape. All I know is that one terrifying hour later we emerge onto land far away from the bangs, guns and enemy troops, to make our way round to the desolate stables where South and I had said goodbye to our own horse a short time ago.

Mary Kelly

England 1917

I place a large bucket on the dairy floor, the handle clanks against the side and the creamy liquid inside waves lazily from left to right. Grateful to stand and rub my back, I look with pleasure at the results of my labour, it feels better that digging things out of the earth. Milking cows is dealing with life; the earth is for death.

I left home a couple of hours ago. The girls should be up and getting ready for school by now. I left them bread and there is even some butter. They're lucky, I had some dry bread on my way as there wasn't enough for all of us. I think I can rely on Enid to share it out and not allow any squabbling.

One of the farmer's sons walks past and gives me a wink. I tut and walk back outside, there's work to be done. He's too cheeky for his own good that one. I don't know his name, there's too many of them in this family to count, let alone name. But I do know I need to keep away from him. He has an easy way, always laughing, he's tanned from being outside all the time and worse, he doesn't go to our church.

'Mary,' he calls to my retreating back.

'Mary,' he insists.

I turn and put my hand up to protect my eyes from the sun.

'Well, I'm busy Sir, if you don't mind.'

'Call me Jim, Mary, I've told you.'

'I have things to do, I can't stop and chat.' I am still reluctant to call him by name, it's too personal. I am employed by his family, there must be a boundary.

'Mary, my dad wants to know if you want some more work,' he pauses and looks at me. 'You could bring the little ones here after school and come back to help out.'

'Doing what?' I mentally count the staff. Everything gets done as far as I can see. 'Is someone leaving?'

'My brother's coming back,' he explains, 'from the war, he's injured.'

I nod.

'We will need some more help in the house, Mam will be looking after Martin.'

'The girls won't be a nuisance?'

'No, there's been enough kids around here over the years.' He grins with secret memories.

'Alright then.' I walk away quickly before he can try to engage me in any more conversation. I feel nervous excitement. Bringing the girls to the farm will be a worry but earning more money will be such a huge relief. We may be able to buy butter every week, maybe even meat occasionally.

I can feel Jim watching me walk away. His smile follows me; I won't turn and smile back. It doesn't do to be friendly. Even to someone who stops your family from starving. Especially to someone who stops your family from starving.

<u>William Jones</u>

<u>Palestine 1917</u>

Harold passes us a cigarette each. He beams. His moustache stretches beyond all belief. I suppress a smile and light up with hands that are still shaking. I look over at South, he is smiling and shaking his head as if he is not sure what is going on.

'We are indebted to you both,' Harold exclaims. 'Our superior officers will be told of your bravery in the dispatches; the country will know what you have achieved.' His moustache stood to attention and waited for my gratitude in return.

Unimpressed, I blow out a long line of smoke and look around for a drink.

'Just get Cooper home and the men to safety.'

'We're moving tomorrow. Make sure the horses are ready.'

I raise my eyebrows.

'I hope they've been fed.'

'They look alright,' Interjects South.

'So do we,' I retort. We look down at our ripped trousers, ragged sleeves, leaky boots and then back up at each other's dirt smeared faces. Somehow, we all manage to laugh. Our deep voices rumble out into the night slicing through the air as confidently as the bullets had just hours earlier.

After a few hours' sleep I get up to find some of the horses have already taken the wounded away and the remainder of the men are getting ready to move.

It doesn't take me long to drag my belongings into order. The horses need my time more than anything. I move slowly round the stable, stroking nervous backs, calming them, reassuring, I wonder briefly if they have any idea what I am saying. I check halters, feet, ears and give them what is left of the rations our original horses couldn't stay alive to eat.

I won't be sad to move on.

....

Part Two

<u>Mary Jones</u>

<u>England 1927</u>

Sarah and little Mary sit in the kitchen, a fire plays in the grate and the kettle whistles good morning as Bill steps into the room. He sits down without greeting us and picks up some bread.

Its darker than our old house but it suits the mood; there's no cheerfulness in this home. Me,

I'm haunted by the ghosts of a previous life and Bill is haunted by the darkness of the war. The girls provide brief glimpses of light, but they know better than to shine here and they fall back into the shadows with relief.

I think back to the day I met Bill at the farm; he had turned up to visit Jim's brother, Martin. They'd been friends in the war. It seemed like an odd friendship to me. There was Bill, tall, angular and angry and Martin, who was shorter and softer with almost feminine ways.

We married shortly after. There was no fuss. It was a relief though, to have someone else to rely on. The terror of the workhouse loomed like a spectre over us. Although not used as frequently as before, I had no family to help, and I knew there was nowhere else for us and then all hope would die. Whereas Bill would always have an income; everyone needed a horse. I quickly learnt what he was like.

I hastily place a mug of tea in front of Bill; he doesn't like to wait.

A knock on the door is followed by a loud 'hello' and Martin limps into the gloom.

Little Mary and Sarah run over to him; drawn as always by his happy smile and twinkling eyes. He's a candle for them and they are drawn to him like moths.

'Let him alone you two,' I grumble.

'Oh they're fine Mrs Jones, honestly.'

'Cooper.' Bill nods towards a chair.

I put some more bread on the table and Martin takes a piece, his delicate fingers gently pulling at the crust, taking little pieces like a bird. Perhaps that is why Bill likes him, with his affinity for his feathered friends. Then I feel unkind. Martin is a nice man, of course that's why Bill likes him. He's just so...so... unlike Bill.

'Mary, Jim says he will be glad to have you back this afternoon.' Martin smiles as he looks over at me. 'He will pick you and the girls up in the cart.'

I nod without speaking. I hadn't worked at the farm for some time; not living in walking distance anymore and being married to Bill but he said I could help at the dairy for a time. Extra money always comes in handy, and the girls need new dresses, something he resents paying for.

'You two will have to behave.' I glare at Mary and Sarah who are playing with Martin's laces. 'Are you listening?'

'Yes mam,' the girls chorus in unison. They dare a quick look at Bill who is chewing his bread and staring into the fire. He comes to and stands up abruptly, rattling the table with his sharp hip.

'C'mon Cooper.' Bill strides out of the door without a

backward glance and Martin follows waving at little Mary and Sarah, he throws a quick nod at me and hurries after Bill.

William Jones

England 1927

We approach the forge under a cloak of early morning mist. One of us straight backed, marching as if by order; the second with an antalgic gait, slightly behind.

I open the door and feel my face and body visibly relax. This is my space. From the sputtering flames to the nest in the pocket of my great coat. This is my true home.

Cooper shuffles to a bench and sits down awkwardly, stretching out his left leg.

I move around the forge preparing for the day ahead, pausing to look at the birds nesting together in my coat pocket. I allow a half smile to pass under my moustache briefly, before continuing with my jobs.

I look over at Cooper, some days I can't believe he is here. The day I left him not knowing how severely he was injured or if I'd ever see him again, haunts me continually. I shiver. Thank God for Cooper. Mary is no comfort. I didn't know what to expect from a wife when we married and although Mary had an independent streak, I'm still responsible for her, and for the kids, along with the ghosts of our pasts.

'We could move in here,' I say, looking round at the forge in appreciation.

'It would always be warm,' laughs Cooper.

The first customer of the day was announced by the sound of approaching hooves. I was glad for the distraction. It didn't do to focus on my mistakes.

....

The fire chatters happily while we share a bottle of brown ale after the last horses have gone.

I drag a blanket off a shelf and lie down. I light a cigarette and watch Cooper rub his leg and stare into the dancing fire.

'Does it ever stop hurting?' I wonder aloud

Cooper shrugs.

'I'm used to it; can't leave it behind can I.'

'A bit like me and Mary.' I said and sat up and reach for the bottle. Realising I didn't know if I had meant Cooper's leg or my life.

'She works hard,' said Cooper, 'Our Jim thinks she's a good 'un.'

A flash of anger shoots across my face as rage rises like boiling lava.

'Does he now; wants to interfere in a man's marriage does he?' Spittle shot from my lips and lands precariously on my moustache as I spit out the words.

'Not like that Bill, don't be daft. He said she's a good worker that's all.' Cooper slides down onto the blanket and looks up at the dirty blackened roof of the forge.

I look down at him and let my anger go with a sigh.

'She wouldn't do Jim no good anyhow; she's hard. He's as soft as that butter he churns.'

Cooper laughs.

'You have a soft side Bill.' He looks into Bill's face, 'the horses, the birds...me.'

I don't reply. I get up, slip off my boots and go to fetch another bottle of brown ale, bolting the forge door on my way back to the blanket.

Mary Jones

England 1927

Sarah was messing about with a teaspoon again, tap, tap, tap. My teeth grind and I worry the nail in the roof of my mouth, with my tongue.

'Get up, do some sewing, or something useful,' I snap. The consonants bouncing like sticks off a drum. Sarah jumps at my tight voice.

'Where's Dad?' she asks even though she knows better.

I reach out and clip her round the ear.

'None of your business that's where; go and get your sister.'

Sarah sniffs and leaves the room; she starts to hum then stops herself.

Seconds later little Mary follows Sarah to the kitchen. They both stand frozen just inside the door frame. I scrub at the table then pause to pick up some bread wrapped in cloth. I hand it to Mary.

'Take this to your Dad, he'll be at the forge.'

Mary didn't hesitate, her skirt flaps dutifully as she disappears from within the frame. She slides away as easily as the discarded photograph that I hide behind a loose brick in the chimney. Checking Sarah has gone into the yard I take it out now and blow off the dust, then allow myself a few seconds' reverie before I slide it back in place.

I tuck the chairs in under the table. There aren't enough spare ones.

'Sarah, get in here and help me clear this table,' I call.

The plates clatter as she conveys them to the sink in haste. I grab a pail and my bush but no matter how I scrub that table, the hopelessness lingers like a greasy stain.

<u>Bernadette St John</u>

<u>England 1927</u>

I brush my hair until it shines; I can see it gleam off the back of my hairbrush. I allow myself a quick glance before continuing. The nuns must not see. Vanity is not tolerated.

I smooth down my simple dress and get up. I place the brush neatly on the sparce old dresser; there is also a small hand mirror and a lace doily on the heavy wood. I made the doily when I first arrived. The nuns were pleased, and I help the little ones with their mending every weekend, I love watching their chubby, clumsy little fingers gradually gain control of the needle and thread. I trace a pattern in the intricate lace for a second then realise I am allowing my thoughts to drift and that won't help at all.

I check my bed is neat and that everything is away; then I look over to the bed nearest to mine and sigh. Teresa. The sheets are hanging halfway to the floor and the blanket is creased chaos. A smudge of dirt insults the white cotton pillow, and her hairbrush is thrown haphazardly on the floor.

I chew my lip as I consider my next action. Tidy it, or go and get her? It's about time she was responsible for her own mess. Ma would've...I stop myself, then my decision is made as I hear the soft pattering of a nun in the corridor. If the room is found in this state, we will all be for it. I swiftly pick up the brush and pull at the bedclothes, covering the pillow and straightening the blanket. It will do for now, I hope.

The nun passes by looking in as she glides down the corridor. The brief glimpse seems to satisfy her. Thank God, I think, then I blush at my blasphemy.

'Wait until I get my hands on that Teresa St John,' I mutter to myself as I finish tidying. I turn the pillow over and satisfied, I leave the room.

S.E LLOYD-WILSON

Katharine St John

England 1927

The ruler cuts into my flesh, searing it with a hot crack of pain. I use every cell in my body to stop myself from flinching.

The nun pauses and looks at my face.

Thwack.

It comes down again. Blood oozes from underneath the well-used weapon. Out of the corner of my eye I see Bernadette walk in. Her face falls when she saw me being punished but she carries on to her seat without stopping.

Finally, a tear escapes from my eyes and makes its lonely way down my face, dripping onto the floor with the smallest of sounds. I know how that tear drop feels. Insignificant, lonely, invisible.

The nun puts the ruler down and stares at me.

'Well?' she enquires.

'Thank you, sister,' I reply obediently. I walk back to my seat, shaking but relieved. I search my pockets for a hanky; my hands come out empty but for the blood leaking its misery on to my skin. Typical.

Seconds later a clean, pressed, white hanky lands on my desk. Bernadette smiles from her seat. I rub at my eyes and face then tackle my hands. There always seems to be fluids to be mopped up here. Tears, blood, urine. Someone was always upset, homesick, hurt, wetting the bed, or worse, wetting in front of people during the day whilst they are being hit or shouted at. It is the little ones I can't bear seeing treated like that. If anyone hurts Teresa, I will get revenge I swear it.

I try to focus on my book, but my eyes feel overwhelmed with the tears I haven't allowed to escape since the war. Those first few weeks here were so confusing. None of us had known why we were here and how long we would be here for.

All that loss and pain and now we've been sent here. This cold, heartless, tomb of a place that was going to do them good, so they were told. Good! I feel as if I'm suffocating; if that is good then the nuns were correct. But I doubt it.

Mary Jones

England 1927

I pull and tug at the sopping wet clothes, my red hands glisten, the sores like rubies and diamonds until I withdraw them and rub them on my grimy apron. I pass a sodden shirt to little Mary who is standing at the mangle.

'Come on girl, let's get this one through quick.' I look around, 'Sarah, this last one can go on the line now.'

Sarah took the partially dried skirt and some large wooden pegs; she has to tiptoe to reach the line, which makes me smile in my more indulgent moments. At least she usually has a peg in her mouth, so she isn't trying to sing whilst she does it.

Little Mary struggles with the mangle and I pull up my sleeves before going to help. The last of the water runs up my arm, tracing a line over my white skin and the dark, purple, bruise. Mary's eyes bulge but she says nothing. I pull the sleeve back down and push her away from the mangle roughly.

'Go and help Sarah.' I turn the mangle slowly and watch the water run away; it fell onto the cobbles and ran free. I wish I could escape that easily.

Bill walked out into the yard, masking the sun with his sour aura.

'Not going to church?' he commented more than

asked.

I laugh. I actually dare to laugh.

'Church,' I announce as if it were a new word to me. 'Do you suppose I can show my face there?' I turn to him so that my black eye was in full view.

He stares at me, meeting my gaze for a second then he turns and walks back into the kitchen.

'That's it, pretend I'm not your problem,' I shout, but I knew I shouldn't.

A snarl reaches out to me from the gloom inside.

'I know you're my problem, believe me. I know.' He threw his mug across the kitchen, then continues with the nearest things to hand. The girls stood at the top of the yard, white faced, big eyed. I shoo them away.

'Go and play,' I say, 'keep out of the way for a bit.'

I leave too; when I can't stand the noise any longer. The farm isn't as close nowadays, I can't walk there for an escape. I wander round the village in a daze.

Standing on the river bridge I look down at the busy water below. The beautiful white froth deceptively hides the darkness and danger underneath. Folks had drowned in there.

I would wonder what drowning is like, but I am doing it every day. Drowning in my own skin. Would drowning in the river be any different?

William Jones

England 1927

The blood drips into the sink. I look around for something I could use to stem the flow. I see a clean hanky on the side and grab it before I make even more of a mess.

'Mary,' I shout towards the stairs. 'Mary.'

Her feet ricochet off the stairs like bullets. She rushes into the room; her face and eyes hard as nails.

'What have you done now Bill?' She snaps.

'Trying to cut the damn bread.' I gesture at the scarlet mess on the table. The crumbs float in the sea of blood like wounded soldiers.
She walks right up to me and breathes in the air around my face. Her sneer comes from her boots and heaves its way onto her face with a weight that could take down a fully grown man.

'Rum,' She states and turns to the table. She picks up the bread and the abandoned knife. After wiping the knife on her apron, she hacks at the bread getting rid of any of the residue of my blood and putting the clean bread out of the way for later.

Her straight back reflects her disgust as she rigidly mops up the bloody mess. When she turns back round, I can see that her apron is flecked with the debris. Our blemished marriage right there on her front.

I thump my good hand down. She jumps, drops her rags and walks out without a word.

I am sitting on the floor with my back against the table when Cooper comes in. I see his shoes first, worn but polished, his dark trousers and odd gait reassuring. He bends down and his dirty blond hair flops down in front of my face.

'Bill.'

I glance up. He lowers himself to the floor beside me, taking care to stretch out his injured leg. He passes me a cigarette which he lights for me. I inhale with pleasure.

"What shall we do Bill?' he asks me, taking a puff on his own cigarette.

'Nothing. We will do nothing,' I shout. I screw up my face; redden like a toddler who can't cope with their frustration. My chest inflates and pain radiates across my rib cage. 'We can do nothing.' An ache flares and my eyes fill with tears which splash down pathetically onto my shaking legs.

Cooper reaches around me and pulls me into him. The reverse of when I comforted him in Palestine. He strokes my hair and shushes me as I gasp and sob. In the background, the bombs fall, the bullets fly, and the horses starve. I slump down into his lap, not caring if I ever get up again.

<u>Teresa St John</u>

<u>England 1927</u>

The chill from the stone walls seeps into my bones. I hurriedly pull on my clothes and pick up my brush. I hear a loud tut from the other side of the room. Bernadette is watching.

She stalks over and grabs the brush which I was using and somehow used to put more tangles in my hair than there was in the first place. Bernadette is not as firm as the Nuns and Bernadette said their Ma had been vicious with hair.

Sometimes I think that I miss Ma even though I can't really remember her, and Bernadette and Katharine tell me she had been strict and not often kind. Still, she was Ma, and I'd like to see what she looked like at the very least.

'Do you think she will ever come back?' I ask turning to look at Bernadette.

Bernadette looks thoughtful, she knows what I mean without asking.

'I don't know. She might not even be alive; turn back around, I haven't finished.

'But she said…'

'I know what she said,' Bernadette snaps. 'I'm older than you and can remember well enough. Don't mind about it now. It won't help.'

I bite back a retort and gulp hard to stop myself from crying.

'What will I do when you leave here?' I manage to ask.

'You'll carry on the same.' This wasn't much comfort. The same, wasn't what I wanted.

Mary Jones

England 1927

When I am alone, I am sure I see a little boy out of the corner of my eye. If I turn, he disappears but I am sure I have seen him.

His dark hair is ruffled, his clothing dishevelled and his face rosy. But he has a question on his lips. One word. Why?

I shiver and walk outside into the sun.

'Good morning, Mary,' Jim shouts

'Morning Jim.'

He squints at me in the sunlight. 'You look a bit pale; are you feeling alright?'

'I'm fine.'

'Sit in the fresh air a while with me.' He winks.

'Ay, I may do that.'

Jim blinks in surprise.

'If only you'd have said yes before, Mary.' His face softens and he leans towards me. 'things woulda been different.'

'No point crying over spilt milk.' But I can't look him in the eye. My mistake is much bigger than spilling milk.

'Fred is visiting today. I'm not sure Martin knows.'

'He spends all his time at the forge with Bill; its not...' I search for the right word, 'natural.'

'They went through a lot together Mary, it creates a bond.'

'You always try to see the best don't you Jim.'

'Why don't you Mary?'

'There is no best. No damn best exists. I just know what is real, that's all.'

If I look hard enough, I can see the girls playing in the field beyond the dairy. Laughing as they run; picking flowers. Then collecting eggs for Jim. They'd had some happiness at least.

'What would be your best Mary? What is it you want?' Jim's voice is like velvet and his eyes tell me they wouldn't accept a lie.

'You know I would turn back the clock; you know what I'd change Jim.' I admit defeat and slump down, beaten.

'You surprised me Mary,' Jim said, honesty at last, 'But I know it was difficult for you.' He looked away, over at the long grass as if he could see the girls in the field too.

'I didn't have a choice,' I said

'You did Mary; you just chose wrong.' He gets up and walks away without looking back. I hear him greet Fred who gives me a wave and continues walking towards the house with Jim.

I knew Jim had wanted to marry me. But I thought he was one for the ladies and I couldn't afford to get caught up with someone who wasn't reliable. Then I met Bill. He was steady, had his forge and a house. It seemed like the sensible thing to do, for the future. So, I discarded the past like it was an old rag.

Teresa St John

England 1927

'It tickles,' laughs Agatha.

I'm laughing too as we rub our bare feet over the

long stalks of grass. The heavenly smell of the dew is a welcome change from the fusty insides of the home.

'Let's see if you like butter.' I grab a buttercup and push it under her chin.

Agatha laughs.

'Now let me try.' I push my chin upwards in excitement.

'Do I?'

'Yes,' she confirms solemnly.

'We'd better put our socks and shoes back on before the nuns come.' I glance towards the dark old building. There's no sign of anyone yet but its best to be safe.

We struggle with our long white socks, then our stiff shoes and long black laces. Agatha pulls a face and mouths a rhyme while she does her lace. She looks up and catches my astonished expression.

'My Ma taught it me.'

'Oh'

'Didn't yours, teach you rhymes?'

I thought hard, pulling at the top of my socks as I did so. Frowning I stood up. 'I can't remember,' I admitted.

Agatha rushed at me and put her little white arms around my neck.

'It's okay,' she crooned, 'Mary's here.'

I stiffened. What on earth was going on?

'Wh, who?'

'That's me,' she beamed. 'It's my real name. What's yours?'

I pulled away, my brow wrinkled, eyes screwed up in distrust.

'My name is Teresa.'

'No it isn't.' Her confident air made me doubt myself.

I had always been called Teresa, hadn't I?

'Mary, Mary,' I muttered to myself.

'Imagine if we both had the same name,' her eyes shone in excitement. Then they darkened with worry. 'Don't let on you know, will you. We're not allowed to talk about it, them, our names...' She drifted off, losing her way as she watched my face.

I ran inside. The corridors seemed never-ending as I rushed through, risking punishment at every corner. It seemed like an age before I got to our beds. They were lined up like obedient soldiers. Just by the door was Bernadette's, then Katharine's, then mine, Teresa's. Except, maybe that wasn't who we were.

Bernadette looked up from her needlework at my flushed sweaty face and nudged Katharine who was still bent over, concentrating.

<u>William Jones</u>

<u>England 1927</u>

Whack, my hand reaches out and slaps her before I can think about it.

She yelps in pain and kicks out with her feet, catching me on the shin. Furious, I grab the nearest pan and strike her on top of her head. Her cry is loud and angry, but she admits defeat.

Mary stands by the grate, wiping her hands on her apron.

'You'll go too far Bill,' She warns in a low voice.

Little Mary shuffles over to the door, her sobs are quiet, hands placed over her head in belated protection. Sarah is frozen at the table. Bread in her hand uneaten; tea in a mug untasted.

'Its my bloody house. Mine,' I roar. My red face leaks rage into the air. 'I can't stand this cacophony in a morning. Bloody women, talking when a man needs peace.'

Mary snatches the pan, where it sat in my hand in as much of state of shock as Sarah. She drops in a lump of lard and placed it on the fire.

A minutes later Mary turns to look at me with a mixture of malice and gloating.

'Well done, Bill.'

She picks up the sizzling pan. The fat lies in a moat around the edges of a Mary shaped dome sitting up proudly in the middle.

Bernadette St John

England 1927

I knew something had changed from the way that Teresa stood in the doorway. She wouldn't have risked running without a serious reason. Nor would she have missed playtime with her best friend.

Teresa stands and stares as if seeing us for the first time. Face red, breath coming in quick bursts. I could almost feel the pounding of her chest.

Katharine puts down her needlework and looks at Teresa too, but she doesn't speak.

No one spoke.

'Ring a ring o roses,' Sang Teresa.

<u>Katharine St John</u>

<u>England 1927</u>

The song shocks us. We haven't sung it in years. We daren't. It held too much of the past.

Bernadette joins in. Her dark curls bob as she sings the rhyme too childish for all of us now but more like home than anything else we have.

I gulp and gape at them both.

Teresa stops singing.

'Why don't you join in…Mary?' she asks.

<u>William Jones</u>

<u>England 1927</u>

Sparks fly and the familiar chink of metal-on-metal echoes through the forge. John is waiting for his horse, and he watches while I work. I feel like he can see right inside me. The sparks of fire, anger and the constant repetitive noise that follow me from ale, to rum, to fist.

'Little 'uns alright Bill?' he asks, 'and your Mary?'

I grunt. I'm not one for small talk.

'Your family alright John?' I must be polite to customers after all.

'Not so bad. Freda said she hasn't seen Mary at church for a long time.'

I pause and look over trying to gauge the other man's meaning. John's smoothly shaved face is calm, his eyes clear, there doesn't seem to be a barb behind his words.

'Busy, John, she's busy. You know how it is, especially with little ones.'
I'll be glad when he's gone. I prefer it if customers leave their horses and go for some refreshment while I am working, instead of getting under my feet.

I try to finish the job as quickly as I can, without compromising the workmanship. I do have some pride.

After he's gone, I check on the birds. They make a right mess; bits of fluff and twig hang out of the pocket of my coat. I don't mind if the little 'uns grow and they're safe. It makes me think of home and my little 'uns. I decide I'll go home later. It's been a few nights. Mary needs to know I'm still in charge I reckon, and the girls need to know it too.

Mary and Sarah. Wouldn't have been my choice of names but she insisted. Beautiful names she said.

I wonder what goes on in her head sometimes.

<u>Mary Jones</u>

<u>England 1927</u>

Deep down I had known that marrying Bill was the wrong thing to do. His demands were unfair, cruel even. But it's amazing what you will do when you think you're faced with starving.

If he was a good husband, I suppose I could live with it. It serves me right really, doesn't it?

The bruises are a familiar enough sight. No one takes any mind now. The girls know not to make a fuss.

I don't go to Church. I don't want the stares, the sympathy, or the gossip.

I lie in bed, awake, wondering if he's coming home or staying at the forge. I hope he stays at the forge. It makes him happy, and we don't have to put up with the effect of his drinking.

The girls are sound asleep. I wander downstairs to make a cuppa. It's a light night and the curtains aren't thick so the moonlight streams in and keeps me company.

I have almost finished the tea when Bill comes in. He looks red, angry, and sour.

'Waiting up to check up on me?' he sneers.

'If that's what you think.'

He walks to the stairs.

'Put that candle out and get to bed.' He orders as he walks past.

I get up heavily and extinguish the flame, following him to the stairs.

He makes slow progress, his heavy boots loud with each drunken step.

I follow, treading precisely on each step with nervous feet.

Just as we get to the last two steps he stops and turns around to face me. He breathes heavily through the curtain of his moustache.

'You chose wrong,' he forced the words out in a deadly rasp.

'Oh ay, what with Bill?' I won't be cowed by him.

He pushes his chest forward, he protrudes out at an unnatural angle, forcing my back to arch and my feet to falter.

'Me,' he says more quietly than he has ever spoken anything. He places his hand on the front of my shoulder. It's a soft touch, almost fatherly. But it's enough.

My arm reaches out, mirroring his movement, my fingers pull at his shirt.

I fall twelve steps, that's all. But it's a lifetime.

Each event bumps into my consciousness as my head bounces and cracks.

Leaving Ireland

The fire

Patrick

War

Hunger

Bill

The girls

The girls

The girls...it echoes in the emptiness.

Bernadette St John

England 1927

I am trusted to look after newcomers now I am training to be a nun. I walk slowly but with pride down the dark corridor. There are two terrified mice like creatures shivering in the entrance; I want to make them feel welcome. I can remember how terrified and confused me and my sisters were when we were left here. First, we had lost our brother, then Da, and then Ma was sent us away. I shivered and pushed it out of my mind.

Their dark curls show them to be sisters. They have matching smudges of dirt on their faces and matching clean tracks where their tears have ran.

'Hello,' I great them with a smile. 'Welcome to St John's. Who are you?'

The oldest one replies but doesn't smile.

'I'm Mary, this is Sarah.'

Sarah looks down at her filthy dress, hair tumbles at her elbows. Mary nudges her.

'We're known by our middle names here. You have saints names I presume?'

'Yes miss,' nods Mary.

'Well then, who are you?' She hesitated then replied.

'I'm Katharine and this is Teresa'

'Katharine and Teresa St John. I know two girls who will want to meet you.'

Enid Bernadette Kelly smiled and led them down the corridor.

John Kelly

<u>1927</u>

All her girls together. I wonder if she can see this from the depths of hell.

Wilson will be there too. He played his part.

My girls are good girls. But oh no, the war hero wouldn't take on another man's children. For all of Mary's faults I never thought she would give up her own offspring. Throw them away, like yesterday's ashes.

It's amazing what some people will do when they're faced with starving. You'll be mentioned in dispatches Mary Jones. Dispatches to the devil.

Ashes in the water
Ashes in the sea
We all jump up with a one two three

Patrick Kelly

1927

I can see me da. There he is. He's smiling and walking towards me. I wave at him. I know he's been watching over my sisters. His job is done now; he can rest in peace.

ABOUT THE AUTHOR

S E Lloyd-Wilson

SE Lloyd-Wilson is a novelist, poet and Teacher of English.

She lives in the Midlands with her partner and youngest child.

PRAISE FOR AUTHOR

Thought provoking. These poems have heart are filled with emotions.

Beautiful wording of which I could relate to! I felt like I had experienced what was being expressed!
I really enjoyed reading it. I highly recommend this book anyone!

BOOKS BY THIS AUTHOR

Music For Mice

A selection of poetry

Slowly I Became Her

A selection of poetry

Continue;

A selection of poetry

Printed in Great Britain
by Amazon